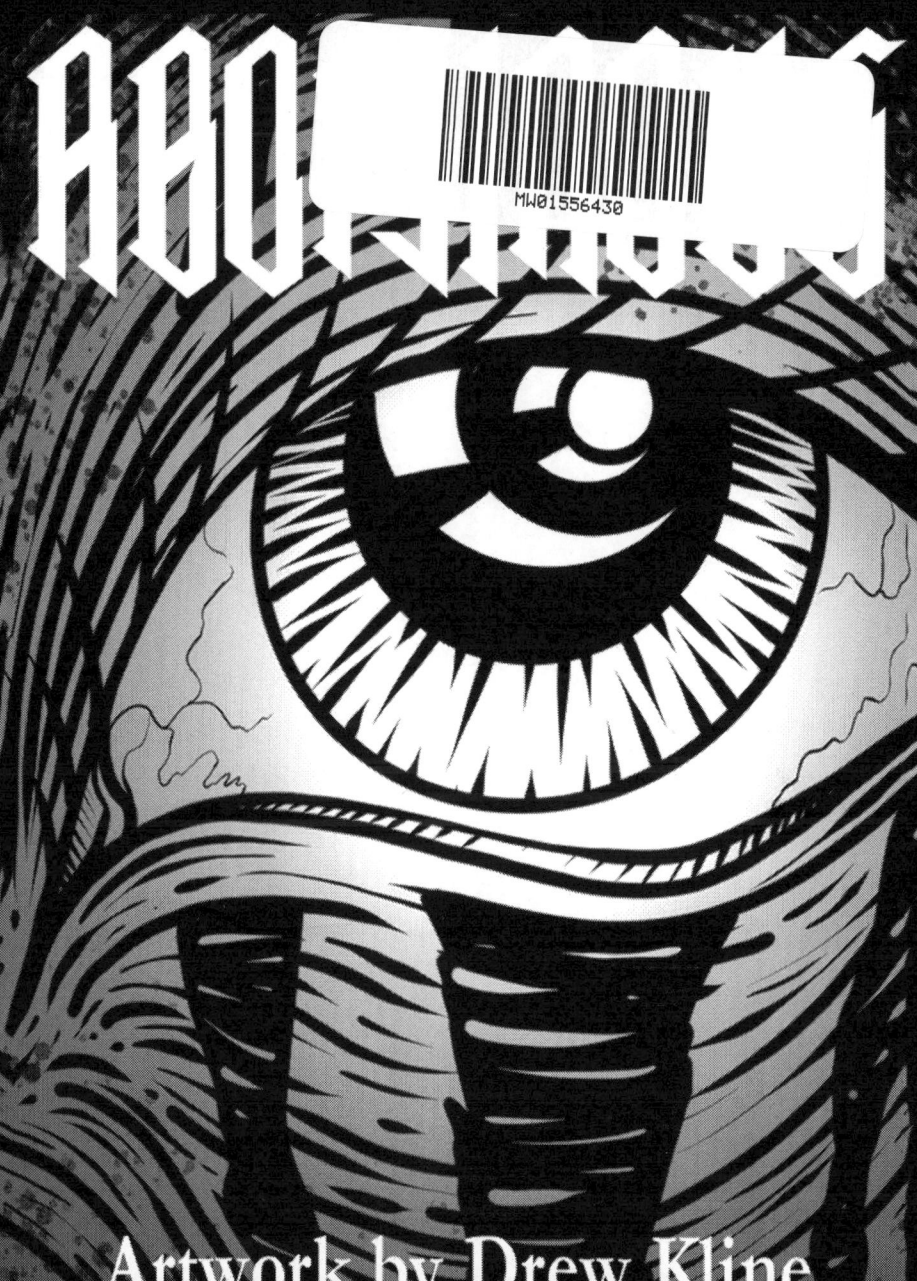

Copyright © 2019 Drew Kline/Matthew Ryan Lowery

All rights reserved.

ISBN: **9781694073396**

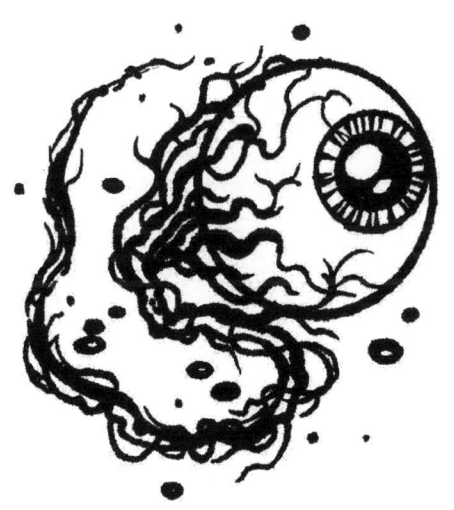

# FORWARD

As the previous owner of Abominous, speaking from merely years beyond the grave,
I regretfully bestowed upon these gentlemen that which could not be tamed.
A tomb of realizations simply meant to haunt and not harm.
Ever walking the tightrope of its readers mind both by neck and by arm.

I myself obtained its torture as a young man almost twenty.
From there I witnessed fifty years of faces, whose color it left empty.
Having personally felt the guilt by which this box of darkness consumes,
One night I rowed deep off the dock and sunk it in a lagoon.

That night I slept as well as I could,
But I dreamt a black figure at my beside stood.
When I woke from my nightmare it had only begun.
My bedroom was flooded. I never met the sun.

So to the poor fellows who Abominous has made itself known,
Please beg my pardon. I do not wish you ill bone.
You are part of its collective and soon you too must face,
The responsibility of hosting a relic from the Devil's bookcase.

I bid you farewell but before I go,
Please follow the rules or Abominous will know.
Be kind to your readers and observant of their shape.
Warn them that the Black Door is their only escape.
The book should not cause harm unless you allow it to make.
For the power of Abominous is anything but fake.

Yours Very Truly,
Augustus Bloodmoon III

Ladies and Gentleman!

Boys and Girls!

Freaks, Meeks, Cowards, and Cheats!

Step right up, if you dare!

See the show critics call,
"Unnerving, distasteful, and depraved"!

A collision course of art and madness for the masses!

The science of desperation commingled with unease!

The show you hoped you would never see!

A terrifying, mind meld of hypnosis and screams!

Both the cure for insomnia and the disease!

We present to you:

**ABOMINOUS**

The worst of your dreams!

Welcome!

Right this way!

Yes, your curiosity craves more?

First let us prepare you for what lies in store.

Abominous does not intend to scare you but simply reveal to your subconscious thoughts.

If you happen to be afraid of your own mind then now is the time to walk.

If you have chosen to move forward then breathe deeply and slow.

Your mind must relax.

Do not fear the unknown.

Behind a red curtain your true self awaits.

Now focus on the red curtain and visualize your fate.

Breathing slowly now.

The red curtain is your focus.

Behind the curtain, is a door.

You are correct, it is a black door. We assure you no tricks. Your thoughts become attuned with Abominous the more you focus.

The black door is safe.

Continue to relax. Continue to focus.

You can always exit through the black door. The black door behind the red curtain.

Through the black door there is a forest. A still forest with a moonlit path.

At the end of the path is a green trunk with a golden lock.

Breathe.

The green trunk with the golden lock is at the end of the moonlit path, through the black door, behind the red curtain.

Now you are relaxed. Now you are open, but the trunk remains locked.

You will need a gold key to unlock the green trunk.

We require compensation for the key.

The gold key that unlocks the green trunk at the end of the moonlit path, through the forest, through the black door, behind the red curtain.

A signature on this line is all we require as payment for your key.

_____

Abominous agrees.

We grant you your key.

Please pass through the curtain and remember that you can always exit through the black door.

CHAPTER 1

# THE CURTAIN

She'll never know the real story.

They'll send a car to our front door.

Say it was an accident.

Hand her a flag and tell her I'm a hero.

I never went to visit.

Cold as stone they laid together,
On a mattress burned, now wet and weathered.
They never woke from the smoke that choked, Their lungs to charred black leather.

The saddest people smile at the simplest of things.

I sailed across the ocean love to find you paradise,
And every night in the stars above I gazed your distant eyes.
The months were long and work was rough but the whiskey's warmth called Winter's bluff,
As I worked away the loneliness,
To find you paradise.

We came ashore in Scotland where seasalt meets the glass,
And I bought a cottage in Oban that was perfect for you lass.
As soon-as-Spring I bought a ring to marry you my dear,
And should this bottle find your door,
Please wear it once a year.

It's calling me. That fucking box.

# CHAPTER 2

# THE DOOR

The door was locked. It was supposed to be.
We practiced a hundred times.

"Abrams, Door check."

"Doors locked Sir."

"Abrams, check that door."

"Doors locked Sir."

"Abrams, open the door."

"Doors locked Sir."

"Abrams, open this GODDAMN DOOR!"

"Doors, locked Sir. I'm sorry."

As the wind gets cool certain ghouls come back to harvest souls.
The stench of rot under your cot marks the dead man's stroll.
The hoots, and hounds, and evil sounds play tricks to rule your mind,
And the crack of bones under your toes sends shivers down your spine.
At the chime of three your sanity will be tickled by their tone,
And come the sun you'll be undone amongst pale gravestones.

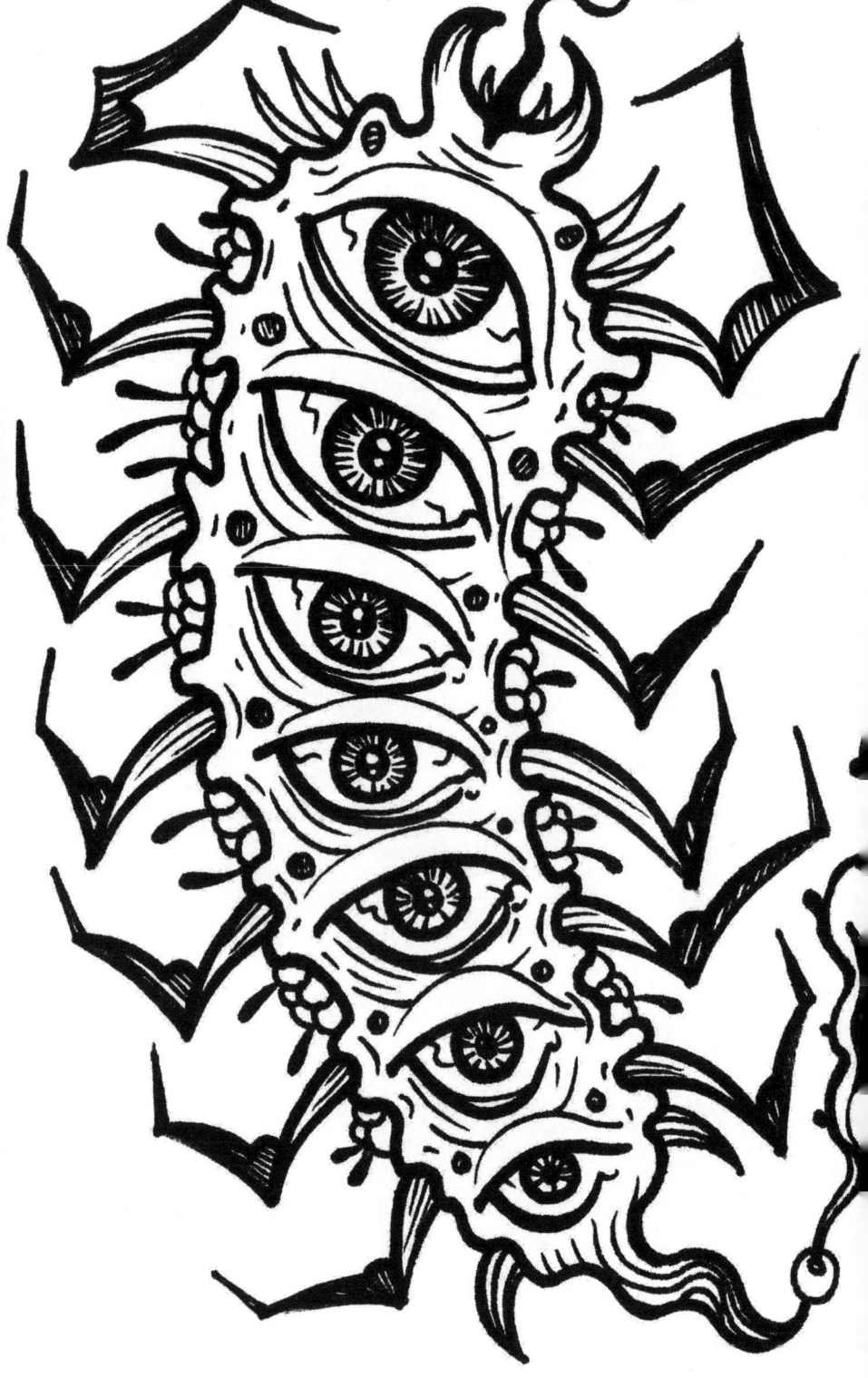

I was frozen.

It just hovered above me.

I still forget where I am sometimes.

Her parents left her all alone
Little Lucy one tenth grown.

In the yard she played till night
With a green balloon to her wrist tied tight.

She ran and jumped and talked and sang
And gave her only friend a name.

She drew a happy face on it
They fell in love and danced a bit.

Then Lucy's mommy called her in,
And cut the balloon free.

I wish I had one friend.

I can't carry this anymore.

CHAPTER 3

# THE PATH

"What the fuck happened?"

"I don't know! We were doing our dailies when we heard a bang. Sounded like glass breaking, but in the vents."

"Why would there be glass in the vents?"

The pills aren't working.

I think they're making things worse.

More than anyone she felt it.
Annoyed by the others so she kept to herself.
Digging her fingernails into her skin.
Never clean enough.
Everyone else is jealous.
Swinging from the ceiling.
Sleeping in a cage.

I don't want to grow up to be myself.

Bleak

As I got older in life I met some really nice people who treated me better than my friends did. I thought they were just acting nice but it turns out that's how they really were. Actually that's how a lot of people were. I pushed them away because I already had friends, and I wish I hadn't.

Music was the best poison I ever drank.

"Ok so...just pull it or I mean...should we say something?"

"Whenever you're ready."

# CHAPTER 4

# THE TRUNK

This thing got in my blood. In my mind.

Molly Goodness and Maggie Milligram,
We're hanging out by the laundry can,
Where happened by chance a change of plan,
That took them on thrill.

Two little chaos pills,
Wrapped up in a daffodil.
They walked until the night got chill,
Then set inside for warmth.

Sinking through the carpet floor,
They drank a glass of record store,
Fought a catchy lyric war,
And fell on off to bed.

When Molly Goodness woke she saw,
Maggie ground her teeth and jaw,
Straight to powder, bone and all,
And froze her head off too.

Molly wandered off and thought
Could have been me, but glad it's not.
She said a little prayer then popped,
Maggie's other pill.

Everything was different before I got sick.

"It's time for your tea."

"Do I like tea?"

"You absolutely love tea darling. You've always been mad for it."

"Oh, well then I can't wait to try it!...Um, what's this?"

"It's your tea."

"Do I like tea?"

Her note said she would see me on the other side. I thought I would, but...where is she?

How many other sides are there?

The horses love running.

I just wanted you to be better than me. My only son. I wanted the world for you. You're no better than the dirt whence you came. They'll come for you and I'll invite them in. You monster. You psychopath.

Don't pick the scab.
Don't pick the scab.
Don't pick the scab.

What is it that makes you feel cold when you're the only person who knows what you're going through?

# CHAPTER 5

# THE KEY

It makes so much sense now. Everything we were taught. Everything we were supposed to be molded into. It was all fake.

This is reality.

This is consciousness.

Now I perceive.

Now I am purified.

My veins are full of thoughts of you,
Red is sorrow,
Hate is blue,
Hell has taught me nothing new,
No tomorrow,
Kiss the noose.

My own children are terrified of me.

Worthless detectives. How many clues do I need to drop. It's like they aren't even trying to catch me. One of the bodies should have been found by now. I hid them practically in plain sight for fuck's sake.

Be careful who you're talking to
I know the devil more than you.

I'm surrounded by so many people but I feel so alone.

I didn't think it was necessary but we decided to tie her down just incase.

He stared at me as they put the second shot in. Then he just looked so tired. I talked to him for about a half hour after he fell asleep.

You're so quiet tonight.

You used to love when I brushed your hair.

My chest hurts.

"I don't know what he wanted, we never talked about it. We don't have a lot of money."

"You could have him cremated and decide what to do with the ashes later."

"I know but I don't know what he wants! I don't want to burn my husband!"

Well then you've made it!

You've made it to the end!
And what did you find in the trunk our dear friend?

Why do you look like you've just lost your head?
A book with blank pages shouldn't offend.

Yes a book with blank pages though some would contend.
Abominous serves each reader their own course of dread.

You seem rather shaken, your hairs stand on end.

Perhaps reading backwards would help your mind to unbend?

Drew Kline holds a Bachelor's degree in both Fine Art and Art History from the State University of New York at Albany. His artwork has been displayed in The New York State Museum, The Albany Center Gallery, and The New York State Capitol, as well as the PAAM Museum and Esmond Wright Gallery in Provincetown, Massachusetts.

He is the owner of Bloodmoon Collective Tattoo and Fine Art in East Greenbush, New York. As a tattoo artist for more than ten years he has won multiple awards including two First Place trophies for Black and Grey from the annual Saratoga Tattoo Expo. His tattoo work has been published in Skin Art Magazine and Tattoodo.

Drew lives in Castleton, New York with his wife and two children.

Matthew Ryan Lowery holds a Bachelor's degree in Political Science from The Nelson A. Rockefeller College of Public Affairs & Policy.

A veteran punk rock musician, he has co-written and released two full length albums, four EP's, and multiple music videos with his bands Radiation Squad, Hijinx, and The Addison Boys since 2001. In 2013 he executive produced a feature length documentary about the band Hijinx which was released through East Grand Record Co. based in Lansing, Michigan.

An avid gamer, Matthew founded Industry Outsiders Gaming podcast and blog site in 2017. He continues to review games on IndustryOutsiders.net.

He has recently finished his first screenplay, "Trouble Bored" a punk rock comedy, and is currently working on his second. He lives in Rotterdam, New York with his wife and pomeranian.

FOLLOW
**ABOMINOUS**
&
**BloodmoonCollective**
ON INSTAGRAM

Made in the
USA
Lexington, KY